P9-CLS-605

Nathaniel Willy, Scared Silly

RETOLD BY Judith Mathews and Fay Robinson
ILLUSTRATIONS BY Alexi Natchev

BRADBURY PRESS • NEW YORK

Maxwell Macmillan Canada • Toronto   Maxwell Macmillan International • New York • Oxford • Singapore • Sydney

Bradbury Press
Macmillan Publishing Company
866 Third Avenue
New York, NY 10022

Maxwell Macmillan Canada, Inc.
1200 Eglinton Avenue East
Suite 200
Don Mills, Ontario M3C 3N1

Macmillan Publishing Company is part of the Maxwell Communication Group of Companies.

Printed and bound in Hong Kong by South China Printing Company (1988) Ltd.
10 9 8 7 6 5 4 3 2

The text of this book is set in 18-point Berkley Oldstyle.
The illustrations are rendered in watercolor.
Typography by Julie Quan

LIBRARY OF CONGRESS CATALOGING-IN-PUBLICATION DATA
Mathews, Judith.
Nathaniel Willy, scared silly / by Judith Mathews and Fay Robinson; illustrated by Alexi Natchev. — 1st ed.
p. cm.
Summary: Nathaniel Willy is scared silly by a squeak in his door, so Gramma must put the farm animals in bed with him for company.
ISBN 0-02-765285-8
[1. Folklore—United States. 2. Stories in rhyme.] I. Robinson, Fay. II. Natchev, Alexi, ill. III. Title.
PZ8.3.M424Nat 1994
398.21'0973—dc20
[E] 92-4052

For Tiger Noah

—JM

For my mother

—FR

For Stefan,
who should not be scared

—AN

Nathaniel Willy and his gramma lived in a creaky old house in the country. Every night at bedtime, Gramma came into Nathaniel Willy's room.

She pulled up the blanket and tucked him in,
Then kissed him resoundingly—*smack!* on the chin.
"Good-night—eyes shut tight," she said.
Then she went out and closed the door.

But one bitter cold night, when Gramma closed the door—*Eeeeeeeek!!* It made a terrible squeak!

Nathaniel Willy got scared. He thought he'd heard a ghost. "*Yow-ow!*" he cried.

Gramma came muttering into the room.
"Don't be a silly, Nathaniel Willy.
My nose is all red and my feet are all chilly!
Now, what if I hurried outside to the shed
And got you the cat and put him in bed—
Would you be scared then?"

"Oh no!" said Nathaniel Willy. "I wouldn't be scared *then*."

So Gramma hurried outside to the shed
And got the gray cat and plopped him in bed.
She pulled up the blanket and tucked them both in,
Then kissed them resoundingly—*smack!* on the chin.

"Good-night—eyes shut tight," she said.

Then she went out and closed the squeaky old door.

Eeeeeeeek!! It made a terrible squeak!

Nathaniel Willy got scared again. "*Yow-ow!*" he cried, and squeezed the cat.

The cat went, "*Scrowll!*"

Gramma came shivering into the room.
"Don't be a silly, Nathaniel Willy.
My nose is all red and my feet are all chilly!
Now, what if I hurried outside to the shed
And got you the dog and put her in bed—
Would you be scared then?"

"Oh no!" said Nathaniel Willy. "I wouldn't be scared *then*."

So Gramma hurried outside to the shed
And got the brown dog and plunked her in bed.
She pulled up the blanket and tucked them all in,
Then kissed them resoundingly—*smack!* on the chin.

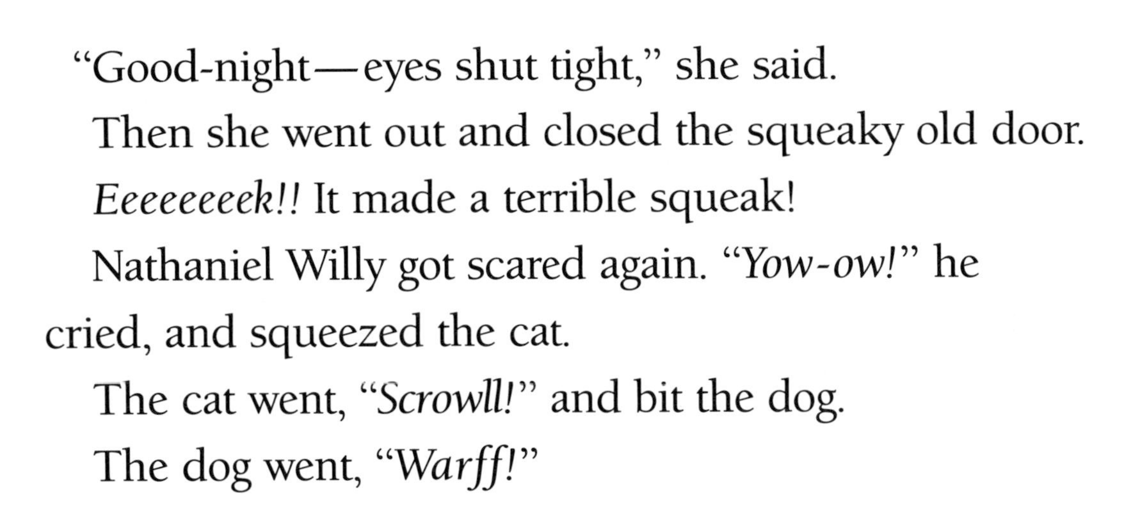

“Good-night—eyes shut tight,” she said.

Then she went out and closed the squeaky old door.

Eeeeeeeek!! It made a terrible squeak!

Nathaniel Willy got scared again. “*Yow-ow!*” he cried, and squeezed the cat.

The cat went, “*Scrowll!*” and bit the dog.

The dog went, “*Warff!*”

Gramma came quivering into the room.

“Don’t be a silly, Nathaniel Willy.
My nose is all red and my feet are all chilly!
Now, what if I hurried outside to the shed
And got you the pig and put him in bed—
Would you be scared then?”

"Oh no!" said Nathaniel Willy. "I wouldn't be scared *then*."

So Gramma hurried outside to the shed
And got the old pig and thunked him in bed.
She pulled up the blanket and tucked them all in,
Then kissed them resoundingly—*smack!* on the chin.

"Good-night—eyes shut tight," she said.

Then she went out and closed the squeaky old door.

Eeeeeeeek!! It made a terrible squeak!

Nathaniel Willy got scared again. "*Yow-ow!*" he cried, and squeezed the cat.

The cat went, "*Scrowll!*" and bit the dog.

The dog went, "*Warff!*" and kicked the pig.

The pig went, "*Snoink!*"

Gramma came shuddering into the room.

"Don't be a silly, Nathaniel Willy.
My nose is all red and my feet are all chilly!
Now, what if I hurried outside to the shed
And got you the cow and put her in bed—
Would you be scared then?"

"Oh no!" said Nathaniel Willy. "I wouldn't be scared *then*."

And so Gramma hurried outside to the shed
And got the fat cow and dumped her in bed.
She pulled up the blanket and tucked them all in,
Then kissed them resoundingly—*smack!* on the chin.

"Good-night—eyes shut tight," she said.
Then she went out and closed the squeaky old door.
Eeeeeeeek!! It made a terrible squeak!
Nathaniel Willy got scared again. "*Yow-ow!*" he cried, and squeezed the cat.

The cat went, "*Scrowll!*" and bit the dog.

The dog went, "*Warff!*" and kicked the pig.

The pig went, "*Snoink!*" and nosed the cow on her belly—right where she was ticklish.

The cow went, "*Moo—moo—mangaroo!*" and shot straight up into the air.

She landed—*wumph!*
The bed groaned . . .
then it rattled . . .
then it wobbled . . .
then it broke:
CRANK—CRRAASHHH!

Gramma came thundering into the room! *"THIS IS JUST PLAIN TOO MUCH,"* she bellowed. "I got you the cat, I got you the dog, I got you the pig, and I got you the cow. I thought that would help, but the bed's broken now. I am out of good ideas. I am going to get the old wise woman who lives down the road."

She went away and came back soon with the old wise woman.

The old wise woman rolled her eyes and shook her head.
"This is no way to go to bed!"

"But there's a ghost in the door!" cried Nathaniel Willy.
The old wise woman closed the door.
Eeeeeeeek!! It made a terrible squeak!
"That's not a ghost," she said. "Your door has a creak, and *that* makes it squeak. And now I'm going to fix it."
She put some oil right where the door was squeaky.
"All done," she said, and went back down the road.

"Silly me," said Gramma. "All this mess for nothing."

She slung the fat cow up onto her back
And put the old pig in a big burlap sack.
With the dog on her left hip, the cat on her right,
She scampered outside and kissed them good-night.

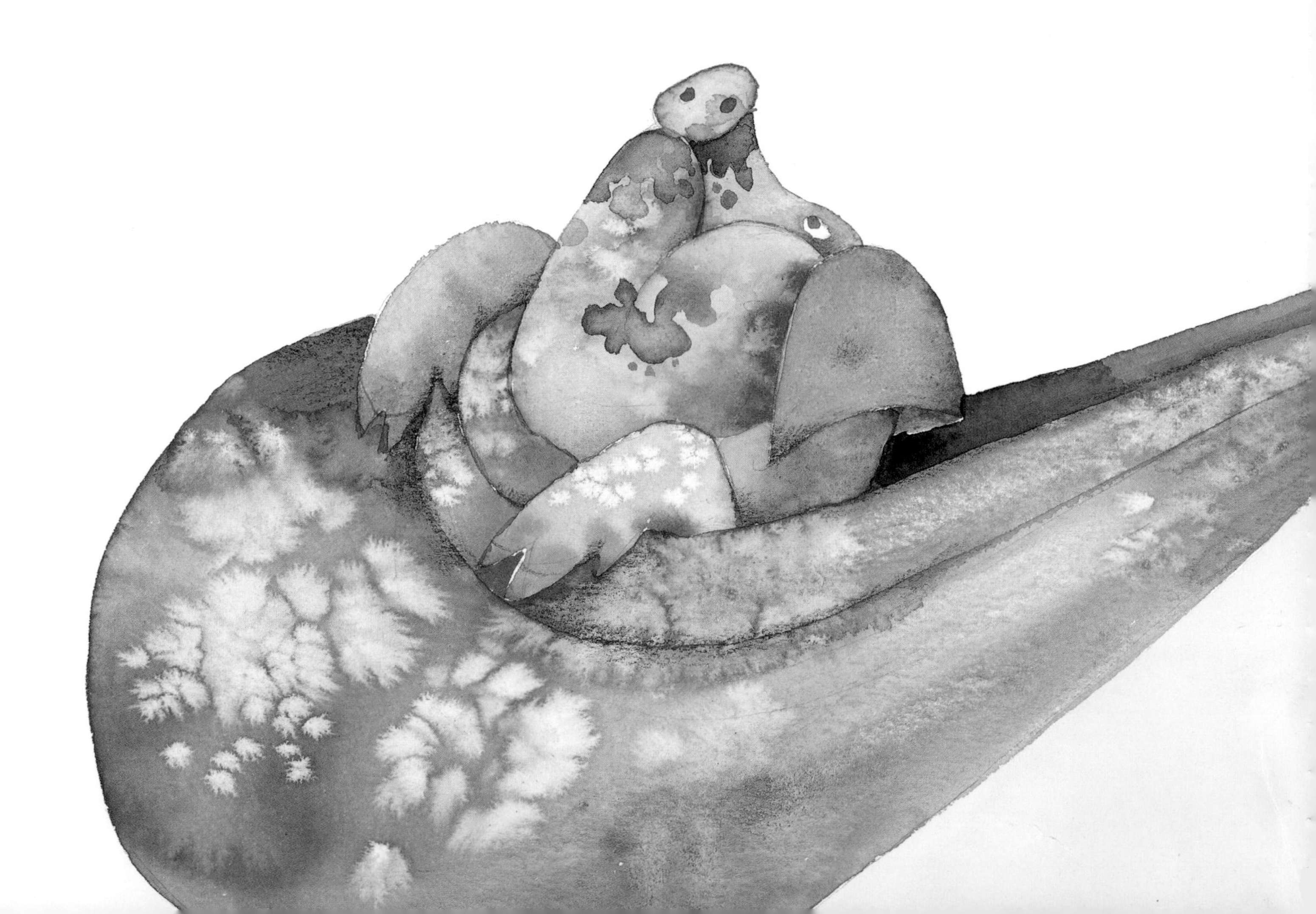

Then Gramma got a hammer and lots of nails. *Bang, bang! Bingo, bang!* Gramma and Nathaniel Willy fixed the bed.

"No more mess," said Gramma.

"And no squeaky door!" said Nathaniel Willy.

Gramma let out an ENORMOUS yawn, and one last time, she put Nathaniel Willy to bed.

She pulled up the blanket and tucked him in,
Then kissed him resoundingly—*smack!* on the chin.

"Good-night—eyes shut tight," she said.
Then she went out and closed . . .

the *quiet* old door.

(*Shhhhhh*!)

AI